A Snowy
Robin Rescue

The Royal Society for the Prevention of Cruelty to Animals is the UK's largest animal charity. They rescue, look after and rehome hundreds of thousands of animals each year in England and Wales. They also offer advice on caring for all animals and campaign to change laws that will protect them. Their work relies on your support, and buying this book helps them save animals' lives.

www.rspca.org.uk

A Snowy Robin Rescue

By Mary Kelly

Illustrated by Jon Davis

SCHOLASTIC

First published in the UK in 2014 by Scholastic Children's Books
An imprint of Scholastic Ltd
Euston House, 24 Eversholt Street
London, NW1 1DB, UK
Registered office: Westfield Road, Southam, Warwickshire, CV47 0RA
SCHOLASTIC and associated logos are trademarks
and/or registered trademarks of Scholastic Inc.

Text copyright © RSPCA, 2014
Illustration copyright © RSPCA, 2014

ISBN 978 1407 14753 6

RSPCA name and logo are trademarks of RSPCA
used by Scholastic Ltd under license from RSPCA Trading Ltd.
Scholastic will donate a minimum amount to the RSPCA from every
book sold. Such amount shall be paid to RSPCA Trading Limited
which pays all its taxable profits to the RSPCA. Registered
in England and Wales Charity No. 219099
www.rspca.org.uk

Printed and bound by CPI Group (UK) Ltd, Croydon, CR0 4YY
Papers used by Scholastic Children's Books are made
from wood grown in sustainable forests.

1 3 5 7 9 10 8 6 4 2

www.scholastic.co.uk

1

Evan loved the last day of term. It was as if the holidays had crept into the classroom. Even though there were ten more minutes of the lesson to go, everyone was chatting and Miss Parker wasn't stopping them. She had paired them all up and asked them to draw Christmas cards. Evan looked down at his picture of a reindeer. *Hmm*, he thought. *It doesn't* look *very much like a reindeer.* He should really start again, but right now, all he could think about was Christmas.

"Evan, you're not even trying!" said his

best friend, Hannah. "You're just chewing your pencil."

"I know," said Evan, sighing. "I'm thinking about all the presents under the tree." There was already a little pile of them, and Evan had sat up last night trying to feel what might be inside each one. The trouble was, his little sister Poppy kept trying to unwrap them. She'd already opened her own presents twice, and Evan had only just stopped her getting hold of his.

"Poppy's getting a set of plastic saucepans," said Evan. "But before she gets through any more wrapping paper, Mum's hidden them in the larder."

Hannah giggled at the idea of presents in the larder. Evan's little sister was only two, but she was very good at getting her own way.

"So what do you think you'll get for Christmas?" Evan asked.

"I've asked for a sketch pad and paints," Hannah replied, without looking up from her drawing. "I really hope I get them."

"I bet you will," said Evan. "Your mum knows how much you love drawing. I've asked for—"

"A new racing-car game for your Xbox?" Hannah finished for him.

Evan laughed. "How did you guess?"

"Because you've been talking about it *all* week," Hannah pointed out.

Evan tried to peek at what Hannah was drawing, but her paper was hidden behind a curtain of hair. He glanced out of the window instead, taking in the heavy, grey skies. "Do you think it's going to snow? Wouldn't it be cool if we had a white Christmas!"

At this, Hannah looked up from her picture, brushing her fringe out of her eyes. "Ooh!" she said, her eyes shining. "It looks like it might! I can't wait to make a snowman."

"And I can't wait to go sledging," said Evan. "I want to see how fast I can go down Shooter's Hill. We've got two sledges at home, so we could have a race!"

Hannah laughed. "OK, I'll race you.

But only if we can have a snowman competition, too."

Evan looked over at Hannah's picture. "Hey, that's really good," he said, catching a glimpse of a sleigh piled high with presents.

"I told you not to look," said Hannah, pretending to swat him with her ruler. "It's not finished yet."

"OK!" said Evan, holding up his hands. "I promise I won't peek." He stared out of the window again, wondering if it was going to snow. He noticed the clouds seemed to have got lower and heavier. *They* must *be full of snow*, Evan thought. And it was freezing outside, too. Everyone had arrived at school this morning with pink noses.

"Finished!" Hannah declared at last.

"Let's swap cards. You go first."

Feeling slightly ashamed now, Evan handed her his picture of a reindeer.

"It doesn't look quite right, does it?" he said.

"You've given it six legs," Hannah pointed out. "And what's that fruit on its head?"

"It's not a fruit! Those are antlers."

"Oh," said Hannah, trying not to smile.

"Let's see yours then," said Evan.

Hannah passed it over. "Wow!" said Evan. It was a picture of a boy in a racing car, zooming past Father Christmas on his sleigh. The boy had freckled cheeks, a snub-nose and a huge grin on his face.

"That looks just like me!" laughed Evan. Hannah had drawn go-faster stripes along the side of the car and a little cartoon robin was holding up the flag at the finish line. Underneath it said, "Merry Christmas Evan."

"Yes, well done, Hannah," added Miss Parker, coming over to take a look. "You can have a merit card next term for that."

Hannah blushed and Evan could tell she was embarrassed. Hannah was always much quieter than he was, and would never boast about her art, so he thought it was great when other people realized how good she was.

"I'm going to keep this," said Evan, putting the card in his school bag. "Then when you're a famous artist I'll sell it for lots of money!" he joked.

Just then, the bell rang and the classroom cheered. "It's the Christmas holidays!" someone yelled.

"Not too rowdy now," said Miss Parker, only just managing to make herself heard over all the voices and the scraping of chairs. "Have a lovely Christmas, everyone. Don't forget your coats and hats."

"Merry Christmas, Miss Parker," the class chorused back, as they all made a dash for the door.

Out in the playground, the very first snowflakes were beginning to fall. Everyone stared up at the leaden skies and the tiny white flakes drifting down. For a moment, everyone was still, as if spellbound by the magic of snow. "Wow!" said Evan. "Just in time for the holidays."

"Let's catch them!" someone cried, and as if the spell had been broken, they all began rushing around, giddy with excitement, snatching at the snowflakes with their gloved hands.

"I've caught one on my tongue," cried Evan proudly.

Hannah stood apart, watching everyone whirl around, leaping and darting after the tiny flakes of snow. Bright woolly hats and trailing scarves made the playground seem alive with colour. Hannah's fingers itched to paint it all.

She held out her black coat sleeves, marvelling at the tiny, perfect snowflakes that landed on them. In the fading light, she could just make out their intricate patterns.

The snowflake game had turned into tag, and Hannah's friend Beth was soon grabbing her arm, urging her to join in. Evan immediately chased after them, making vrooming noises like a racing car.

"Got you!" he cried, quickly catching up with them.

They carried on playing even as the school playground emptied. Parents arrived, picking up their children, calling out for them to zip up their coats and find their hats.

"Come on, Evan," said Hannah, as the teachers began shooing everyone gently out of the gates.

"Do you want to come back to mine?" asked Evan. His house was only three doors away from Hannah's, so they spent most of their time in and out of each other's houses. "We've got hot chocolate and mince pies at home."

"Deal!" said Hannah, grinning.

Evan spent a few moments hunting around for his scarf, then followed Hannah towards the gates.

"Merry Christmas!" he called out to his friends.

"Merry Christmas!" they called back. "Bye, Evan! Bye, Hannah!"

They started walking quickly through the snow, Evan looking forward to tucking into one of his mum's mince pies.

Hannah was still looking all around, loving how the snow changed everything. She spotted a squirrel ahead of them, scattering small showers of snow as it leaped from branch to branch.

"I expect the squirrel is looking for food, too," she said. "Perhaps he's trying to remember where he buried all his nuts."

"I'm glad I don't have to remember things like that," said Evan. "I'd be a hopeless squirrel!"

Hannah giggled, while Evan flung out his arms. "I, Evan Smith, declare that this snow is here to stay," he announced.

"Really?" said Hannah. "And how would you know?"

"Look at the treetops and the fence posts! *Everything's* starting to get a layer of snow." He looked at Hannah, his eyes gleaming with fun.

"Enough for a snowball fight?" asked Hannah.

"You read my mind," said Evan.

As he spoke, they both reached down and began scooping up snow in their hands. Evan finished his snowball first, sending it flying towards Hannah. It landed with a small thud against her padded coat.

"I'll get you for that," laughed Hannah.

Soon they were running down the street, throwing tiny snowballs at each other.

"Oh!" cried Hannah suddenly. "Look up!"

"Is this a trick to get one down my neck?" asked Evan.

"No," laughed Hannah. "It's really not." She held up her hands to show she had no snowballs. Then, together, they both gazed up at the sky. The flakes of snow were fatter now, swirling down from the grey clouds, sparkling where they caught the light of the street lamps.

"I love snow," said Hannah, grinning. "It feels as if Christmas has already started."

2

They took a turn down a little side road, that led to the cul-de-sac where they lived. It wasn't far now, so they ambled along slowly, wanting to make the most of the first flurry of snowflakes.

Evan had starting chatting again about the racing-car game he wanted, while Hannah let her gloved fingers trail along the top of the wall, tracing patterns in the light layer of snow.

"Wait a moment," said Hannah. She stopped to draw a cartoon robin on the top of the wall. This time she added a twig of holly for him to perch on.

"It's like snow graffiti," said Evan. He added a six-legged reindeer beside the robin and Hannah laughed. "Draw something else," Evan urged her.

Hannah looked around for inspiration, then spotted a fat black cat in the window of the house opposite. He was curled up behind the curtain, looking very pleased with himself. As Hannah looked at him he opened his green eyes and blinked at them.

Hannah quickly did a snow-sketch of him on the wall, next to Evan's reindeer.

"You've got him perfectly," said Evan. "He looks all warm and cosy. Actually, that's why snow is so great. You get to have fun playing outside in it, and then be all warm and cosy inside."

"I know!" said Hannah. "And right

now I can't wait for one of your mum's mince pies. Hers are the best."

"That's what comes of having a mum who used to work as a chef," said Evan, proudly. "I think she misses it a bit now she's looking after Poppy. But on the plus side, it means we get amazing food at home!"

As they walked into the cul-de-sac, away from the noise of the cars, everything became oddly quiet and muffled. The street lamps above them had taken on an eerie glow, the yellow lights shrouded in a halo of snow.

This is going to be the best Christmas ever, thought Evan.

Up ahead, they could see the lights were shining from the houses and Hannah could just make out the Christmas trees in people's windows, the shining baubles and the twinkling fairy lights. "Everything looks like a Christmas card, doesn't it?" she said.

"I hope it keeps snowing all night," Evan went on. "Then we'll wake up to fresh snow everywhere. That's one of my favourite things – running through fresh, crisp snow before anything else has touched it."

"Apart from animal tracks," Hannah pointed out. "I remember it snowed a couple of years ago, and we saw these sweet little bird tracks all over our back garden. There were fox footprints, too."

"Talking of tracks," said Evan, pointing back the way they'd come, "look at ours!"

Hannah glanced down at their footprints, meandering side by side along the pavement.

"Let's make a trail!" said Evan. They began running around in circles, weaving in and out of each other, admiring the marks they left behind. It had gone so quiet, all Evan could hear was the satisfying crunch of his feet sinking into the fluffy snow.

"If anyone was trying to follow us," Hannah pointed out, "they would be very confused. Hey," she added, "watch this." She carefully placed her feet in Evan's footprints, so that her own disappeared from view.

"Neat," said Evan. "Not as good as this though!" And he started walking backwards. "This would really confuse someone."

"Watch out!" Hannah cried, having to stop herself from laughing as Evan collided with a bush. All the freshly fallen snow on the leaves landed directly on his head, making him look like he was wearing a blobby white hat.

"Don't laugh," said Evan, shaking off
the snow.

"I'm trying not to," said Hannah. But a
small giggle escaped from her lips, and she
found that once she'd started laughing,
she couldn't stop. Then she realized that
Evan was making an enormous snowball.

"OK, OK, I've stopped laughing!" she
protested, as Evan took aim.

Then, in the silence that followed, she heard a faint noise coming from the hedge nearby.

"Wait!" she said, suddenly. "Can you hear that?"

"What?" asked Evan, still holding on to his snowball. "If you're trying to distract me, it's not going to work."

"No, really," insisted Hannah. "I can hear a sort of chirping noise."

Evan dropped his snowball and began to listen. "Yes!" he said. "I can hear it, too."

Together they approached the hedge in the direction where the sound was coming from. "I think it's this way," said Hannah.

They tiptoed forward, trying to be as quiet as they could. They were nearly at Evan's house now.

"Oh, it's gone quiet," whispered Evan. "I can't hear it any more. Perhaps it's flown away. Hot chocolate here we come," he added. "Let's go inside. My feet are frozen, and I'm not sure I can feel my fingers any more."

He began heading in the direction of his house, but Hannah didn't move.

"Evan, wait!" she said, gesturing to him. "Please, come back!" She didn't know why, but she had a funny feeling about the bird, as if it were somehow calling to her. There was something distressing about the sound of its chirping. "Are you sure you can't hear it?" She paused for a moment, straining her ears, then she heard the chirping sound again, fainter than before, but definitely nearby. Evan must have heard it too, as he turned and walked back towards the hedge.

Together, they crept forward, following the chirping sound. Hannah could feel her heart beating fast in her chest, as if she'd just run a great distance, though she wasn't sure why. With trembling hands, she reached out and parted the snow-laden leaves. At first it was hard to see anything in the dark winter afternoon, but then she shifted her position slightly, and the light from the street lamp beamed down on them.

"There it is!" she breathed. On the ground, where the bottom of the hedge met the pavement, was a little robin. She heard Evan gasp beside her.

"A lovely Christmas robin," Hannah whispered, as they gazed at it. "Isn't he beautiful?" she added, admiring his glossy red breast. The robin had his head cocked to one side, clearly watching them

with his shining black eyes. His head and back were pale brown, just like the bark on the plane trees that lined their street.

"I've never seen one this close before," said Evan.

"Oh, look," said Hannah, still keeping her voice to a whisper. "He's got a little white spot under his red breast. Isn't that cute?"

"And he's so tame," marvelled Evan, as the robin chirped at them again. "I can't believe he's not flying away."

"We have a blackbird like that in our garden," said Hannah. "He always comes down to say hello when my dad's gardening. Sometimes he just sits on my dad's spade and watches him. I think he hopes my dad is going to dig up some worms for him."

"That sounds really cool," said Evan. He looked back down at the robin. "My granddad told me once that robins are really territorial, always defending their own little patch. But I can't believe it looking at this one. He doesn't look like he'd get into a fight."

Hannah laughed. "I think that's mainly in winter, when there's less food around. I love how they stay with us all through the year, though, and don't fly away like other birds."

"What do you mean?" asked Evan.

"You know!" said Hannah. "Like the swifts and swallows that come for summer, and then fly back to Africa in winter."

"No way!" said Evan. "All the way to Africa? I never knew that. How come you know so much about birds?"

"Probably for the same reason you know so much about computer games," said Hannah, smiling. "I just like them."

They got up to go, but Hannah put her arm out to stop Evan. "Don't you think it's odd," she said quietly, "that this robin hasn't moved *at all*?"

"You're right," said Evan. "It's still chirping, but it does seem weirdly still. Do you think this one's been injured?"

"It's hard to see now the light's fading," said Hannah. "I can't really make out its legs at all."

They bent down again to take a closer

look, moving as carefully as they could so as not to alarm it.

"It's *still* not flying away," said Evan. "I think that's really strange. Maybe it's broken its leg or something."

"Oh no," said Hannah, her voice an urgent whisper. "Evan, the poor robin – I've just realized it's completely stuck.

3

"What do you mean it's stuck?" asked Evan, frowning.

"Look," said Hannah. "It's standing on a piece of cardboard and it can't move its legs. It must be stuck to the cardboard in some way. And there – do you see? Its tail feathers are stuck down, too. It must be caught in some type of glue."

Evan reached out to touch it, to see if he could help.

"No!" said Hannah quickly, reaching out to stop him. "I think we should get help."

"Then let's run back to my house," said Evan. "It's closer. Mum will know what to do."

Evan looked at the robin one more time, memorizing the exact spot where they had found it. Then he and Hannah took off, racing down the snowy pavement, their coats flying out behind them. Luckily, Evan's house wasn't far away, but they still arrived panting for breath at the door.

Hannah noticed the holly wreath hanging on the door and the fairy lights in the window. But she couldn't think about Christmas now. All her thoughts were focused on the robin.

They burst through the front door.

"Mum! Mum!" called Evan, running down the corridor without stopping to take off his shoes. Hannah realized they were trampling snow all over the carpet, but it didn't seem important right now.

"In here!" replied his mum, from the kitchen. "You took your time coming home from school," she added, as they came through to find her. "Have you been enjoying the snow?"

She looked up as Evan and Hannah burst into the kitchen. Evan realized she was tidying up after cooking. There was flour everywhere, and his little sister, Poppy, was sitting on the kitchen counter beside his mum, playing with a piece of pastry.

"What's the matter?" asked his mum, taking in their flushed faces, their brows creased with worry.

"Oh!" began Hannah. "We've found a robin. . ."

". . .and we think it's stuck," finished Evan, still breathless from their run. "It's out by the privet hedge at the end of our road. It's on a piece of cardboard. It can't move and it keeps calling out, as if it's really distressed."

"Right," said Mum, immediately springing into action. "Let me come and take a look." She wiped her floury hands on her apron, lifted Poppy down and went briskly to the hallway. As she put on her warm fleecy coat she had a quick look out of the window. "It's snowing really heavily now," she noted. "We'll have to wrap up warm."

She passed Hannah a spare scarf, gave Evan a woolly hat and zipped Poppy into her snow suit. "Let's all put on boots, too," she said. "Your shoes look sopping. Hannah, you can borrow an old pair of Evan's. They're just under there," she added, pointing to the shoe rack under the stairs.

Hannah pulled out the boots while Mum helped Poppy into hers. "Red boots," said Poppy proudly, stamping up and down on the floor.

"They're lovely," said Hannah, smiling at her. She thought Poppy looked a little like a robin herself, in her red snowsuit and boots.

"Red's her favourite colour," said Evan. "Because of her name."

"Poppies are red," said Poppy, very seriously.

"Just like you," added Hannah.

"Right . . . house keys, phone. . ." said Mum, tapping her pockets. "We've got everything. Let's go." She turned to Hannah as they went out of the door. "Do your parents know where you are, love?" she asked.

"No," said Hannah. "Although they'll just think I'm here as usual."

"I'll ring them as we go, then. I don't want them worrying."

They hurried out on to the street, Mum managing to carry Poppy in one arm and use her other hand to phone Hannah's mum.

Evan was glad of his woolly hat. The snow was coming down in thick, fat flakes now, and it was deep enough to cover the tops of his boots. "Oh no," he said suddenly. "You don't think the robin will be buried under the snow, do you?" He looked really worried.

"It was under the hedge, remember?" said Hannah. "I think it'll be sheltered there — at least a little bit."

"Where did you find it?" asked Mum, when they reached the hedge.

"It's just here," said Evan. "I remember because it was near the street lamp."

"See robin! See robin!" cried Poppy excitedly.

"Hush now," said her mum, jiggling her about on her hip. "Oh yes, I see it." She put Poppy down on the ground. "Evan, hold on to her hand, will you, while I take a look, and can everyone stay back? I don't want to alarm the robin even more."

Evan kept a tight grip on Poppy as he felt her strain forward, longing to get closer to the bird.

"Want to see!" she cried.

"The robin is really shy, Poppy," said Hannah, keeping her voice to a whisper. "We have to be really quiet, or it'll get scared."

"OK," said Poppy, doing a stage whisper back.

Mum was crouching down low next to the robin.

"What do you think, Mum?" asked Evan. "Can you see what's happened to it?" He glanced over his mum's shoulder as he spoke, taking in the robin's tiny body against the blanket of snow. Its black eyes were still shining brightly and it let out another little chirp.

His mum stepped back before

answering, to give the robin some space. "You're right," she said. "It does look like it's stuck to that piece of cardboard. It seems really nervous, too."

"What do we do now?" asked Hannah.

"I think we should phone the RSPCA," said Mum. "I'm sure they'll be able to help. They have trained inspectors who specialize in rescuing animals." She moved further away from the robin as she spoke, and the others followed her.

"I hope someone will be able to come out," said Hannah, looking anxious. "It's getting quite late."

"It's all right," said Mum soothingly. She was looking up the RSPCA on her phone. "It says here it's a 24-hour helpline."

"Wow!" said Evan. "I never knew about that. That's like an emergency service for animals."

They waited while Mum's call was connected. Evan began making a mini snowman for Poppy, to keep her occupied.

"Hello," said Mum, as she was put through. "I'm calling about a robin we've found near our house. It seems to be trapped on a piece of sticky cardboard. We were wondering if you'd be able to come and help?"

Everyone waited while Mum listened to the reply. Hannah felt relieved when she saw Mum's face break into a smile. "That's great," she said, giving their address. "Yes, yes, I've got that. Thanks again."

She put down the phone. "Good news," she said. "They're going to send out one of their inspectors to take a look. In the meantime, she says we mustn't touch or approach the bird."

Hannah nodded. "I understand," she

said, taking another look at the robin. It was reassuring to be able to see it, but she knew they had to keep their distance.

"Did they say how long it would take for an RSPCA inspector to come?" asked Evan.

Mum shook her head. "Only that they'd be as quick as they can. I've given them our address so they know where to go."

Evan was still looking anxiously at the robin. "Hannah's right," said his mum. "The robin is sheltered under the hedge, at least. And there's nothing we can do now except wait. Let's all go inside and wait there with a hot chocolate. The mince pies will be ready soon, too."

Evan and Hannah exchanged glances. "If it's all right, Mum," Evan said, "I think Hannah and I would like to stay with the robin. I promise we won't go near it. It just feels wrong to leave it alone."

"Please," added Hannah. "We'll be warm enough now you've wrapped us up in extra hats and scarves."

"OK, if you're sure?" said Mum. "I can see it means a lot to you. I'll ring your mum again when I get back and let her know what's happening. But make sure you come in if you start to get too cold."

"We promise, Mum," said Evan, smiling at her.

His mum gave him a quick hug. "Well done for finding the robin," she said to both of them. "Come along, Poppy. Let's go in."

"Want to stay, too," said Poppy, gripping on to Evan's hand.

"No, love, it really is too cold for you," Mum said, scooping Poppy up in her arms. "And it's very important we go in and check on our mince pies. We don't want them getting burnt."

Poppy nodded. "Check pies," she said, very seriously.

"We'll bring you some out when they're ready," said Mum, as they headed in.

"Thanks, Mum," Evan called after her.

"I hope the RSPCA inspector gets here soon," he said, after they'd gone. "*We're* OK in our coats and hats, but the robin must be freezing."

"It's got its feathers," Hannah reminded him. "They'll be keeping it warm. And it would be out in the cold anyway, at this time of year."

"That's true," said Evan, feeling cheered at the thought. They waited in silence for a little while, then Evan looked up, smiling, to see Poppy and his mum coming back towards them. Poppy was clutching a little basket of mince pies.

"Pies!" Poppy announced proudly.

"Thanks, Poppy," said Hannah, passing one to Evan and taking another for herself. "They look delicious."

"Are you sure you don't want to come and wait inside?" asked Evan's mum, giving an exaggerated shiver against the cold.

Evan shook his head. "No thanks, Mum. We're fine, really."

"OK. I'll keep an eye on you from the window."

As his mum and Poppy headed inside again, Evan realized how quiet it was out in the dark. No one came along the street and the air was thick with falling snow. The only sound was the cheeping of the tiny bird.

Evan and Hannah soon finished their mince pies, and Evan was glad of the warmth it gave him. He felt guilty though, at being able to keep his own tummy full while the robin was stuck out in the snow.

"I'm glad we're waiting out here with the robin, aren't you?" Hannah asked him.

"Yes," agreed Evan. He turned back towards the robin. "We're not going to leave you," he said to the little bird. "We're going to stay right here and look after you."

4

As they waited, a cold wind whipped around them, sending the snow in giddy spirals to the ground. Hannah blew on her gloved hands to keep them warm, while Evan flapped his arms and hopped about like a bird.

"I wish I knew how to reassure the robin," said Hannah. "It's hard when we have to keep our distance."

"I know," agreed Evan, "but I'm sure the RSPCA were right on the phone – we'd only upset it by going closer."

They could still hear its faint chirps and

the robin seemed to be watching them, following their movements by tilting its head.

"Help is coming, little robin," said Hannah, softly. "We'll get you out of here."

She looked over at Evan as she spoke. "I know it can't understand me," she went on. "I just wanted to do *something* to reassure it."

"Maybe it's just good that we're here," said Evan. "We can make sure nothing comes to attack it, like a cat or a dog."

There was the sound of a car and they both peered around the corner, only to see a neighbour pull up and park in one of the driveways.

"Oh!" said Hannah, disappointed. "I thought that was going to be the RSPCA."

"I'm sure they'll be here soon," said Evan.

He looked back at the robin to check how it was doing.

"I can't believe how tiny it is," said Evan. "Robins seem bigger when they're flying around. Now I'm looking at one standing still, it seems so small and fragile. Do you think it's a baby?"

"I don't *think* so," Hannah replied. "I'm pretty sure baby robins are all speckled and brown. They don't get their red breasts until they're older."

"Maybe it's a mother. I hope she hasn't got a hungry nest of babies waiting for her."

Hannah couldn't help smiling a little. "Evan! No bird is going to have a nest in the middle of winter. They won't start until spring."

"Oh," said Evan, feeling foolish. "I suppose it would be a bit cold for baby birds. And hard for their parents to find food for them. It's funny, all the things you never think about. And I should know more about birds, really. My granddad loves birdwatching. He's always trying to get me to go with him, but I've never been that interested before."

Suddenly, they heard the sound of car tyres slowly crunching through snow. Both Hannah and Evan looked up, their eyes dazzled for a moment by the beam of headlights. A large white van was drawing up, with RSPCA written on the side in large letters.

"Oh, they're here! They're here!" Hannah whispered excitedly, not wanting to startle the robin.

They both raced over to the van as it

pulled up alongside the kerb. A woman
jumped out, wearing a sturdy pair of black
boots, dark navy trousers and a dark navy
jacket, with an RSPCA logo on its pocket.
Evan could see her curly brown hair,
poking out beneath her cap.

"Hi," she said, smiling and holding
out her hand to them. "I can guess who
you two are – you must be the children
who found the robin? I'm Courtney, the
RSPCA inspector."

"Yes," said Evan, shaking her hand and feeling very grown up. "I'm Evan and this is Hannah. We found it on our way back from school. Shall I show you where it is?"

"Please," said Courtney. "Have you been waiting out here in the cold for me?" she added, as they walked towards the hedge.

Hannah nodded. "We wanted to stay with the robin," she said, "but we made sure we kept our distance."

"Well, you did the right thing," said Courtney, "and I'm really glad you called us."

By now they'd reached the hedge, and Evan lowered his voice to a whisper. "There it is," he said, "right next to the hedge, on the ground. It's standing on a piece of cardboard and we think it must be stuck to it. It can't move its legs at all!"

Courtney bent down to get closer to the robin, moving very gently and quietly. The winter sun had faded by now, so Courtney took a torch from her pocket and shone it at the robin's feet. "Oh," she sighed. "I thought it might be that."

"What is it?" asked Hannah. "What's it stuck to?"

"It's a glue trap," she said, still examining the robin. "The robin's lost some tail feathers – you can see them caught in the glue here – and I'm afraid these ones are going to be damaged."

"That sounds horrible!" said Evan.

"It is," Courtney went on. "People use glue traps on mice and rats, but they're not very humane. The animals get their feet stuck in the glue and then can't escape. And the trouble is, other animals get stuck to them, too. I wish people wouldn't use them – or at least not just throw them out like this."

She walked over to her van and pulled out a cardboard box, lined with a towel. "I'll have to take the robin back to the RSPCA centre to treat him," she explained. "It's not something I can do here. I need a controlled environment and it'll be less stressful for him at the centre."

"Do you think you'll be able to get it out of the trap?" Hannah asked anxiously.

"I hope so," Courtney replied. As she spoke, she very gently lifted the robin, still attached to the cardboard, and placed it inside the box.

Evan watched it all, breathlessly. "How will you do it?" he asked, as Courtney closed the lid.

"We'll use oil to unstick the robin,"

Courtney explained, carefully carrying the box back to the van. "The oil is bad for the bird's feathers, but it's the only way to remove them from the glue. Then we use washing-up liquid to clean the oil off the feathers."

Evan and Hannah glanced nervously at each other. Both were thinking how hard it was going to be, watching Courtney drive away with the robin, not knowing if the little bird was going to be OK or not.

"I really hope you manage to free it," said Hannah, tightly crossing her fingers as she spoke.

Courtney smiled at her. "It doesn't look as if too many feathers have been damaged, so hopefully this little guy is going to be OK."

"It's gone quiet now," Evan pointed out. "It was chirping a lot when we first found it. Do you think that was a distress call?"

"Probably," said Courtney. "It was lucky you heard it. And it's a good sign, too, that it was still calling. If the robin was really weak it wouldn't have been making any sound at all."

Evan nodded, grateful for the reassuring tone in her voice.

"And it'll be all right in that box?" asked Hannah.

"These are the boxes we use to transport animals to the centre," Courtney explained. "The towel will stop the robin from slipping about. And see here," she added, pointing to the little holes along the side, "these are for ventilation so the robin has fresh air to breathe."

"That's good," said Hannah, trying to smile. "Is it far to the centre?"

"It is quite far. It's not ideal to put the robin through a long journey, but it'll need treatment if we get it out of the trap, so the centre is the best place. First we'll have to make sure we've got rid of the oil, as it stops a bird from being able to regulate its temperature properly. It may not be able to fly for a little while either, until all its feathers grow back."

"Poor little thing," said Evan.

"We'll be feeding it up," Courtney

added, on a more cheerful note. "This little bird will enjoy getting lots of tasty seeds and juicy mealworms."

Courtney shut the doors to the van and gave them both a big smile. "I'd better get going," she said, "so we can start work on freeing the robin as soon as possible. It is very fiddly," she admitted, "and it will be traumatic for the robin, but he'll be looked after by professionals. So I really want to thank you both. By finding that robin and calling us, you've most likely saved that little bird's life."

She climbed inside her van, gave them a wave and started up the engine. Evan and Hannah watched as she turned the van around in the cul-de-sac, then began heading out again. They ran after her a little way along the pavement, waving until she was out of sight.

They walked back towards Evan's house,
noticing how thickly the snow lay over
the ground.

"I really hope the robin's going to be
OK," said Hannah, taking one last look at
where he had been.

"Me, too," said Evan, a frown creasing
his brow. Then he smiled at Hannah,
as if trying to cheer them both up. "I
don't know about you, but I'm freezing.

I definitely think it's time for that hot chocolate!"

"Deal!" said Hannah. "What a start to the Christmas holidays — snow *and* a robin rescue. I just hope they manage to save him. That really would make it the perfect Christmas."

5

"Wheeee!" Evan shot down the hill on his toboggan, loving the feel of the wind on his face, the trees, the snow, the faces all flying past in a blur of speed.

"I'm coming up behind you," shouted Hannah. "I'm going to win."

"Oh no you're not," Evan called back, crouching low. He sped down the last part of the slope and reached the bottom first. "I am the winner!" he crowed.

Hannah just laughed. "OK, you might have won this time, but let's have a rematch."

They turned back up the hill again, dragging their toboggans behind them. It had snowed all through the night, and now it was as if the whole world had turned white. The branches on the trees drooped low, laden down with snow, and the hill was covered with children, all laughing and calling to each other as they flew down its snowy slopes. Some people had brought proper wooden toboggans, others were zooming down in makeshift sledges made from plastic lids or trays.

Evan's parents and Poppy were waiting for them at the top of the hill.

"Well done, you two," Evan's mum called out. "That was super-speedy."

"Poppy's turn!" cried Poppy, trying to take hold of Evan's toboggan.

"Oh no you don't," said Dad. "You can go down on my knee, but you're not going down on your own."

"Hooray!" cried Poppy. "Go down now!"

Dad gave an exaggerated sigh and pulled Poppy on to his knee.

"Poppy really loves the snow, doesn't she?" said Hannah, turning to Evan's mum.

"Well, it's the first time in her life she's seen it, so it's pretty exciting. Actually, to be honest, I'm excited, too. Now, who's ready for lunch?"

"Me!" cried Evan. "My tummy can't stop rumbling."

"Must be the cold," said Dad. "I'm starving. Let's go for lunch at the café at the bottom of the hill."

"Can we toboggan down?" asked Hannah. "I still have to beat Evan!"

"Go on then," laughed Mum. "We'll see you there."

Hannah and Evan sped down the hill towards the café. Hannah tried to copy Evan's move, leaning forward so the wind whistled over her back. She thought at one point she was going to win, but then he pulled up beside her and they finished in a draw.

"I wanted to beat you!" laughed Hannah.

"Never!" cried Evan. "I'm the champion."

"Just you wait, Evan Smith. I'll beat

you yet," Hannah teased.

They left their toboggans outside the café and strolled inside to wait for the others.

"What an awesome day," said Evan, as they found a table. "Snow and toboggans and the Christmas holidays. What more could we want!"

"I know," Hannah agreed. "There is one thing though – I wish I knew how our robin was doing."

As soon as Hannah mentioned the robin, Evan was aware of a feeling that had been nagging him all morning – like a TV programme he never saw the end of, or a book left unfinished.

"Me, too," he admitted. "I kept thinking about it all last night, as well. It doesn't seem right, not to find out what happened to it."

"I did some research on the Internet," Hannah went on. "I read up on robins. I found out that they eat earthworms and spiders and insects, but in winter they eat fruit and berries. And did you realize the feathers on their breast are actually orange, not red? I'd never thought about that before."

"Nor had I. I'm always going to think of them as being red though! Robin redbreast sounds much better than robin orangebreast."

Hannah laughed. "That's true," she said.

"I looked up robins, too," Evan confessed. "I suppose finding out about them made me feel like I was still in touch with our robin. Wouldn't it be amazing if we could see it again?"

Before Hannah could reply, the others all piled into the café. "What will it be?" asked Evan's dad. "Hot chocolate all round?"

"Yes, please," said Hannah.

"And me!" added Poppy, who hated being left out of anything.

"So," said Dad, once he'd ordered their hot chocolates. "I want to hear all about this robin you found."

Evan and Hannah exchanged glances. As Mum filled Evan's dad in on all the details, Evan couldn't help admitting how they felt.

"We really want to know if the robin is all right," he said once Mum had finished. "We're worried about it."

"We don't even know if it made it out of the glue trap," Hannah added. "And even if it did, Courtney said the robin had lost some of its tail feathers. Do you think that means it won't be able to fly again?"

"I'm sure the RSPCA are taking very good care of it," said Mum. "The robin is in the best possible hands."

"I know," Evan replied. "It's just that we got so involved in its rescue. It's hard not knowing what will happen to it."

They were interrupted by the arrival of their hot chocolates. Evan grinned when he saw they were piled high with marshmallows, melting deliciously into the chocolate to make an amazingly sweet goo.

"Where's mine?" demanded Poppy.

"We didn't think you'd manage a *whole* one," laughed Mum.

"You can share mine," offered Hannah.

As Poppy took a spoonful of marshmallow, Hannah brought the conversation back to the robin. "So," she said, rather hesitantly, "do you think the robin will be OK? I kept thinking about it last night, before I went to sleep."

"I know it's worrying," said Dad, kindly. "But the main thing is that you called the RSPCA and you watched over it, so you did everything you could."

"And Courtney did say we may well have saved its life," added Evan.

"Exactly," said Mum, seeing Hannah's anxious expression. She gazed around the café for a moment, as if trying to think of something to distract them. "Now," she went on, including all of them in her smile, "did I ever tell you any of the old wives' tales about robins?"

Evan shook his head and grinned at his mum, realizing exactly what she was up to. "No," he said. "Go on then, tell us."

"Well my dad, your granddad, always used to say that if you saw a robin redbreast on Christmas Day, you had to make a wish before it flew away."

"Oh, I like that one," said Hannah. "My mum said that if a robin is the first bird you see on Valentine's Day, then you're going to marry a sailor!"

Dad pulled out his phone. "I'm going to see if there are any more on the Internet," he said. "Here we go – if you see a robin singing out in the open, it means sunny weather. But if you see it singing under shelter, it means it's going to rain."

"That's a good one, too," said Mum. "Are there any more?"

"Oh yes," said Dad, winking at Hannah and Evan. "If you rescue a robin from a glue trap, you will get all the Christmas presents you want."

"Very funny, Dad," said Evan. "Does that mean I'm going to get my computer game?"

"You'll have to wait and see," said his mum, smiling at him.

Evan laughed along with them, but under the table he was crossing his fingers. As much as his parents tried to distract him, he couldn't stop thinking about the little robin. He'd give anything to know it was getting better.

6

A few days later, Evan was woken by his mother gently shaking him awake. "Wake up, sleepyhead," she said. "We've got a very special adventure planned for you today."

For a fleeting moment, he realized he'd been dreaming about the robin again. He tried to remember what had happened in his dream, but his memory of it was vanishing as he took in his mum bustling about his room, attempting to clear up the racetrack on the floor.

"It's not more Christmas shopping, is

it?" Evan groaned. "I don't think I can take any more. Not after yesterday and the clothes shopping."

"It's not clothes shopping," laughed his mum. "This is something you'll really enjoy. Now hurry up, get dressed and come and have some breakfast."

Evan jumped out of bed. He put on his clothes as quickly as possible, managing to put his trousers on back to front in his excitement. Then he ran down the stairs. Poppy was already at the breakfast table, her doll propped up next to her, making a strange mush out of her cereal.

"Mornin'," she said, waving her spoon at him. Pieces of cereal went flying across the table.

Evan deliberately chose the chair furthest from Poppy.

"Good decision," said his dad. "I've already been covered in cereal this morning."

Poppy ignored them both and began feeding cereal to her doll.

"Will *you* tell me what the surprise is?" Evan begged.

"No, I can't!" laughed his dad. "Otherwise it won't be a surprise."

"Me come too?" asked Poppy.

"Not today," said her dad, ruffling her hair.

"*We're* going to stay at home and make a gingerbread house," said her mum.

Poppy seemed happy with this and went back to feeding her doll.

"Just give me a clue!" pleaded Evan. "Have I ever been there before?"

"No, you haven't," replied his dad, "and that's the last question I'm answering. Here's some toast. Now eat up as we have to go soon."

Evan munched down his toast, his brain in a whirl.

He was just opening his mouth to beg for more details when the doorbell rang. "I'll get it!" he cried, jumping up from his chair. He ran to the door, hoping it might reveal the surprise.

"Oh!" he said. Hannah and her dad were standing on the doorstep. Hannah was looking just as confused as he was.

"Are you coming on the surprise trip, too?" Evan asked.

Hannah nodded. "Does that mean you don't know what it is either?" she whispered.

"No one's telling me anything!" Evan whispered back. He stepped aside as he spoke, smiling at Hannah's dad as he let them into the house.

"Great!" said Evan's dad, clapping his hands together. "All present and correct. We can set off."

Evan noticed his parents were grinning from ear to ear, as if they'd done something they were really pleased about. Whatever this surprise was, his parents obviously thought it was a brilliant idea.

"How are we getting there?" Hannah asked.

"In the car," replied Evan's dad. "I'm driving you both."

"Cool," said Evan, high-fiving Hannah. They clearly weren't going to find out where they were going beforehand. He might as well get in the spirit of the adventure.

Hannah hugged her dad goodbye, then she and Evan sat together in the back of the car, gazing out of the window as Evan's dad navigated the snowy roads out through the town and into the countryside. The narrow roads flanked by buildings were gradually replaced by fields, all covered under thick layers of snow.

"There's even more snow out here, isn't there?" said Hannah.

Evan nodded. He hadn't really been taking in the view. He was too busy trying to work out where they were going.

"Oh, look – a field of horses!" said Hannah. "I feel like I really am in the countryside now. And there's a flock of starlings over there."

Evan craned over to Hannah's side of the car to take a look.

"Every time I see a bird, I can't help thinking of our robin."

"Me, too," confided Hannah, just as Dad turned off the road into a driveway.

"Here we are," he said.

"Wow!" gasped Evan and Hannah together. The sign outside said "RSPCA Wildlife Centre".

"This is awesome!" cried Evan.

"Is this where our robin was taken?" asked Hannah, desperate to know. "Are we going to see it?"

Dad turned round, smiling at them. "It is," he said. "And it really is a special treat as members of the public aren't usually allowed. But the RSPCA agreed to it just

on this occasion, because of your help in
the robin rescue."

"Double wow!" said Evan. "And that
must mean our robin is doing OK, too,
don't you think? They must have got him
off the glue trap."

"Let's go in and find out," said Dad.

They walked up to the entrance and rang
the bell. A woman came to meet them. She
was dressed in a black jacket lined with
a red fleece, with RSPCA embroidered

on the pocket. "Hi," she said, smiling at them. "You must be Evan and Hannah. I'm Karen, the manager here."

She shook hands with them all. Dad introduced himself, too, and then Karen led them out of the cold and into the warmth of the building.

"We've heard all about how you helped rescue the robin," she went on. "Would you like to see how he's getting on?"

"Yes, please," they said at the same time.

"Is our robin really a 'he'?" asked Hannah. "I always thought of him as a boy."

"Yes, he really is," laughed Karen. "We'll take you to see him first, and then if you like you can have a tour of the centre."

"That sounds amazing," said Evan.

"How is he?" asked Hannah quickly. She couldn't bear not knowing any longer. "Did you get him off the glue trap OK? Did he lose many feathers? Will he be able to fly again?"

Karen held up her hands, as if to ward off the barrage of questions. "He's doing really well," she said, smiling at Hannah. "But you'll soon see for yourself."

Hannah smiled back at her, relief flooding her face.

"Our robin's OK," she mouthed to Evan. In reply, Evan gave her a huge thumbs up.

They walked past the front office, where a smiling woman with glasses waved at them. Evan saw that there were pictures of animals all over the walls and lots of posters up about feeding birds in winter.

"I'll tell you what," said Karen. "As we go, I'll take you through what's been happening to the robin since you last saw

him. So first," she went on, pointing to
a computer in a little cubbyhole off
the passage, "we logged him in here. All the
animals that come into the centre go on
the database, and are given a case number."

"What's the number for?" asked Evan.

"It's so we can compare similar cases
and look up how they've been treated."

"That's clever," said Evan's dad.

"Well, we get around a hundred and
fifty different species a year, so we need
to keep track of them all," explained

Karen. "And just through here," she added, leading them down a long corridor, "is the examination room. That's where we take animals as soon as they arrive, to assess them. We weigh them, to see if they need feeding up, and decide on the treatment plan."

Evan peered in at the little room. It looked a lot like a vet's surgery, with an examination table, a weighing machine and a small cupboard full of equipment. He imagined what it must have been like for the robin arriving here, and how terrified he would have been. "Is this where you removed him from the glue trap?" he asked.

"Yes," said Karen. "Although it wasn't done by me, but one of our veterinary nurses. She cleaned off the rest of the glue and then washed off the oil with washing-up liquid. It's a really complicated job, and should only be done by a trained professional, so it was brilliant that you rang us."

Hannah and Evan exchanged smiling glances.

"After that," Karen went on, "he was put under a lamp to dry."

"He must have been really scared," said Hannah.

"Small birds do get very distressed," agreed Karen. "That's one of the risks of treating them. But your brave little robin made it through."

Evan and Hannah grinned at each other at that. They liked how Karen had referred to the robin as "theirs".

"And if you'd like to follow me through here," she said, leading them back out into the corridor, "I'll show you where he went after that."

"Wow," said Evan's dad, "he's been on quite a journey."

Karen stopped outside another room filled with small cages with wire fronts. "This is where we put our animals to stabilize after their examination. The whole experience can be very stressful for them, so we like to put them somewhere warm and quiet."

Hannah and Evan peered inside. They saw a row of incubators and some more open wire cages with a couple of pigeons crouching down on the floor of their cage. Each animal had a little piece of paper clipped to the front of the cage, saying what they were and why they had come in. Then Evan spotted a cage at the back with a pillowcase over the top.

"What's that for?" he asked quietly.

"That's for a blackbird that's just come in," said Karen. "He was quite traumatized, so we've covered his cage to block out some of the light and noise. Now," she added, "I'll show you to the next room and you'll get to see your robin at last."

Evan could feel his heart beat faster with excitement as Karen stopped outside another door, with a sign on it that read "Bird holding room".

"In you go," she said, holding open the door for them.

Evan and Hannah stepped inside to see lots of little aviaries, each one with green twigs strung up and birds perched inside. They passed two more pigeons and a blue tit, then Evan caught sight of a robin in a cage. The breath caught in his throat as he took in the familiar beady eyes, the red breast with the little white patch beneath. . . "Is that our robin?" he asked in a rush. "Is it really him?"

"It really is," said Karen.

"I can't believe it!" cried Evan. He stepped towards it. "Look, he's hopping around," he said. "Isn't it amazing, Hannah?"

Hannah shook her head, her eyes wide with wonder. "He's like a different bird," she said in a hushed voice.

The robin looked cheeky now, not scared. He regarded them with his bright black eyes, his head cocked slightly to one side.

"Can he fly?" asked Hannah.

"Yes, he can fly. He's lost a few tail feathers, but luckily that doesn't seem to have affected his flight," Karen replied. "That's why we've moved him to this cage — so there's more room for him to flit about. We've added the leaves, and a little perch, to make him feel more at home."

For a moment, they didn't say anything. They just stared and stared at the little robin, thinking how lucky they were to be able to see him again.

"Chirpy little fellow, isn't he?" said Dad, breaking the silence.

Hannah laughed. "He is now," she said.

"Oh!" she added, peering closer. "I can see where some of his tail feathers are still missing."

"You're right," said Karen, "but the good news is that they'll grow back."

"How long will that take?" asked Evan.

"A while," admitted Karen. "Not until his moult, in midsummer, which is when all the feathers are replaced. But the really important thing is that he can still fly."

"I can't believe how much he's changed," said Hannah, unable to take her eyes off the robin. "It was so horrible the way he was before – not able to move. And now I'll be able to remember him like this. All chirpy and hopping!"

Then Evan turned and looked at Karen. He had a question to ask and he had to know the answer. "So, will you be able to release him back into the wild?"

"We will," said Karen. "Very soon."

Evan and Hannah grinned at each other.

"He'll spend another day in this room, and then we'll move him to one of the outside aviaries, so he can have more room to fly around and acclimatize to the chillier temperature."

"That's the best news *ever*," said Evan.

Dad smiled at him and squeezed his shoulder. "Thanks so much for showing us the robin," he said to Karen. "The kids have been really worried about him. I think you just about made their Christmas."

"Definitely," said Hannah, grinning.

"What other animals have you got here?" asked Dad.

While Karen chatted about the other animals they were looking after, Evan and Hannah couldn't tear their eyes away from the robin. It was amazing seeing him this close up. Before, they had only just been able to glimpse him in the light from the street lamp.

"Look," said Evan. "He's got a funny toe on each foot that points backwards."

"Most birds have those," giggled Hannah. "I think it helps them grip on to their perches. And look," she carried on, "he's not just brown all over, is he? I can see lovely blue-grey feathers around his breast."

"Oh, yes," said Evan. "And have you noticed the way he can't stop moving?"

They laughed as he hopped over to his food bowl and began pecking away at the seeds, spreading them everywhere.

"He's fast when he moves, isn't he?" Evan pointed out. "And I can see him breathing – the way his little chest keeps puffing in and out."

"Yes, he's very active now," said Karen, overhearing their conversation. "It was a really good sign that he never lost his appetite."

"What do you feed him?" asked Evan.

"Mini mealworms and something called prosecto, which is mashed up insects. We give him a mineral supplement, too. And of course he's got a little water bowl in there as well. We won't release him until we think he's ready to find his own food, but that'll be any day now."

"So," Karen went on, "would you like

to come and see the other animals?"

Evan and Hannah both nodded, but Evan couldn't help feeling sad to be going so soon.

"Goodbye, little robin," whispered Hannah, still lingering by his cage. He looked straight at them. "Do you think he remembers us?" she said.

"I hope so," said Evan. "I wish we didn't have to leave him though. I wish this wasn't goodbye."

Karen seemed to notice their reluctance. "Well," she said, after a moment's pause, "it does seem a shame you won't get to see the last stage of this little robin's journey. . ."

Evan and Hannah both waited, holding their breath.

"How would you feel about being there when he's released?" Karen finally said.

"For real?" gasped Evan.

"Really, really?" asked Hannah.

Karen laughed. "I'm pretty sure we can arrange it," she said. "We'll be doing it close to your house, so it shouldn't be that hard to organize. And it would be a lovely thing for you to see."

"That would be the best thing *ever*," said Evan.

Hannah felt like leaping up and down on the spot, and only just managed to stop herself, realizing it might surprise all the animals. "Thank you! Thank you!" she said.

"Well, we've got you to thank for calling us about the robin," said Karen. "Come on, now. I've got even more animal treats in store for you."

After that, they saw a fox who had been found cowering on a doorstep, a whole flock of swans paddling about in an outdoor pool, a hedgehog curled up on a pile of hay and two pet rabbits.

"We don't usually have pets here," Karen explained. "These two were found hopping down a high street! We're just looking after them until they can go to an animal centre for rehoming."

"I wish I could take them home," said Hannah, as one rose up on its back legs, twitching its nose inquisitively.

She looked pleadingly at Evan's dad. "Don't give me that big-eyed look," he said. "I'm not walking out of here with a couple of rabbits. I don't think your parents would be too happy about that."

"It could be my birthday present?" said Hannah, half-teasing. "I'm sure Mum and Dad wouldn't mind."

"You'll have to ask them!" said Evan's dad, chuckling. Then he turned to Karen. "You'd better warn me if there are any more cuddly animals coming up."

"Well, I've saved the best for last," said Karen. "Although you definitely won't be able to take these home with you. . ."

She led them to another outdoor pen, with high-walled sides mounted with wire. Hannah and Evan peered over. "Wow!" gasped Evan. "Are those really. . ."

"Yes," laughed Karen. "They're really seals. We often get them this time of year. There's three of them — young seals that have been washed ashore by the winter storms. They end up here if they've been found injured or underweight. We feed them up and look after them before returning them to the sea."

Evan couldn't take his eyes off them. They looked almost human, their sleek heads bobbing above the water, their eyes

huge and black. "What kind of seals are they?" he asked.

"These are common seals," said Karen. "Aren't they amazing? They can swim just a few hours after they're born, usually around June or July. Sometimes we get grey seals, too. They're the ones that look all white and fluffy when they're born. They stay on land for the first month or so of their life, then take to sea once they've grown their waterproof, adult fur."

"They're gorgeous," whispered Hannah. "I could spend all day looking at them. Do you mind if I take some photos?"

"Go right ahead," said Karen.

After that, they were allowed one last look at the robin, before it was finally time to go home.

"I think I'll remember this day for ever,"

said Hannah sleepily, from the back of the car.

"Me, too," said Evan. "Our robin and a fox, hedgehogs and seals . . . even Christmas isn't going to top that!"

7

Evan and Hannah waited anxiously at the window for the RSPCA van to arrive. It had been three days since their visit to the RSPCA centre, and today was the day they were going to release the robin back into the wild. Evan wasn't going to miss it for the world. Hannah had arrived just after breakfast, and they'd been waiting at the window ever since. Evan's mum had taken Poppy to the shops to buy some last-minute extras for their Christmas lunch, while his dad waited at home with them. He'd already made lots of jokes about Hannah living here now.

"The RSPCA said they'd be here *sometime* this morning," Dad pointed out. "You could be waiting at the window for a long while. And the roads are still covered in snow, remember, so that might delay them."

"I know," said Evan, who was almost hopping up and down with excitement. "But we can't miss this. That would be terrible!"

"I'm sure they'll knock on our door first to let you know they're here. Why don't you come and sit down?"

"But the moment I sit down, they'll come," Evan insisted.

"Nonsense!" laughed Dad.

Evan was just sitting down when Hannah cried out, "They're coming! They're coming! I think that's their van pulling up now. Yes, it is! Can we go out and see them?"

"Of course you can," said Evan's dad, as the van parked up outside their house. "But make sure you wrap up warmly first. It's freezing outside."

Without another word, Hannah and Evan began throwing on their coats and stuffing their feet into their wellies as fast as they could. Then they rushed outside to greet the RSPCA officers, who were just climbing out of their van. Evan instantly recognized Courtney, who was wearing the same uniform as before. This time she had a man with her, with copper-coloured hair that reminded Hannah of the feathers on a robin's breast. He waved to them as they approached.

"Hi, Courtney," said Evan shyly. "Do you remember us? Evan and Hannah?"

"Of course I remember you two,"
said Courtney. "And this is Greg," she
added, gesturing to the man beside her.
"He's going to be helping us with
the robin release today. He's one of
the wildlife assistants at the RSPCA
centre."

As Greg shook hands with them,
Courtney went around to the back of
the van to open up the doors. "How did

you enjoy your trip around the RSPCA centre?" she asked.

"It was brilliant," said Evan. "We saw a fox and swans and seals. My favourite part was definitely seeing our robin again though."

"We'd been really worried about him," added Hannah. "It was great to see him again. And to see him freed from that horrible glue trap."

"Well, he's a fighter," said Courtney. "We were really lucky that he didn't lose any more feathers, and it looked like he was in good condition before he got trapped. But you two definitely helped save his life. If he'd been stuck in that trap any longer, it could easily have been a different story."

"I'm just glad we were there," said Hannah. "It was so lucky. Actually, that's what I'm going to call the robin — Lucky. What do you think, Evan?"

"I was thinking more Senna or Hamilton," joked Evan.

"We're *not* naming him after a racing driver," said Hannah.

"Well, I think Lucky is a perfect name for him," said Courtney, laughing. "I'll just get him out of the van now, and then we can get ready to release him."

As she spoke, Evan's dad came out of the house and introduced himself to Courtney and Greg. "You can be very proud of these kids," said Greg. "They did exactly the right thing."

"I am," said Dad. "I also feel like I know everything there is to know about robins. These two haven't stopped talking about him since they found him."

"Are you going to stay and watch him

being released, Dad?" asked Evan.

"No, I've got to go inside and finish off some work. Besides, this is your moment. You two have earned it."

He turned and started heading back towards the house. "And then you can come in and tell me *all* about it," he called over his shoulder. "I'm looking forward to every single detail."

Greg chuckled. "It really does sound like you've been telling him a lot about robins."

"I expect it makes a change from racing cars," said Hannah, giving Evan a nudge.

Then they both fixed their attention on the back of the van, waiting for the moment Courtney would lift out the robin.

"There he is!" said Evan, as Courtney

turned, a carrier in her hand.

"Is that him?" asked Hannah, rushing towards her as she carried it on to the pavement.

Courtney nodded in reply, and Evan and Hannah peeked inside to see their little robin. He was just visible through the holes in the cardboard. Evan felt a tingle of excitement that they were going to watch this last part of the robin's journey back to freedom.

"I'm always surprised by how tiny he seems," said Hannah.

"Small but strong!" added Evan. "Where are you going to release him? Are you going to do it where we found him?"

"Very nearby," said Courtney. "We always try to release birds near to where we find them, unless there's a very good reason not to. That way, everything will be familiar to him – all his landmarks and food spots and the territory he's no doubt been defending. We've picked out a hedgerow, just in the field behind the street, which we thought would be the best place. The robin can use it for shelter during the winter, and he'll be able to find lots of food there as well."

"Can we come, too?" asked Evan, as Greg and Courtney started heading towards the field.

"Of course," said Courtney. "It wouldn't be right without you. Just make sure you stand back a bit when I release him, and make as little noise as possible."

They followed Courtney and Greg into the field. Hannah and Evan kept glancing at each other as they walked. They both knew this was the perfect end to the robin's story, but it still felt strange to be saying goodbye to him.

As soon as they reached the hedgerow, Courtney set down the bird carrier and looked around.

"We'll release him here," she said, "as it's so close to where we found him. And it's ideal as it's got lots of gardens nearby brimming with food." Then she looked over at Evan and Hannah. "Would you like to take a last look at Lucky, before I release him?" she asked.

"Yes, please," said Hannah. "I actually feel quite sad now it's time to say goodbye. I mean, I know it's the best thing for him," she added quickly, "but it's odd thinking we'll never see him again."

"You never know," said Greg. "I wouldn't be at all surprised if he found his way into your garden, especially if you hang up a feeder, or spend time digging around in the soil."

"That's true," said Hannah, her face brightening.

"We wouldn't know it was him though, would we?" said Evan. "I'm not sure I'd be able to tell him apart from the other robins."

"Actually you would," said Courtney. "We've put a little ring around his foot, so the RSPCA can track him. That way, if he ever gets into difficulties again, we'll know who he is. So if you find a robin in your garden who's been tagged, you can be pretty sure it's Lucky."

She slowly began to open the top of the box and Evan and Hannah peered inside. "Oh!" gasped Hannah. "He's so sweet." Lucky's two little feet were planted on a tea towel, and he was looking at them curiously with his beady black eyes. They looked shiny and bright, and he'd fluffed out all the feathers on his breast. The only things that showed what he'd been through were the ring around his foot and his tail, which was still missing a few feathers.

"And Lucky can definitely fly, can't he?" asked Evan.

"He definitely can," said Courtney. "We wouldn't be releasing him if we didn't know he was ready for it. He's been flitting around his enclosure at the

RSPCA centre and greedily gobbling up lots of insects and worms."

"Why are his feathers all fluffed up?" asked Hannah. "It makes him look just like a robin on a Christmas card."

Courtney smiled. "That's to protect him from the cold," she explained. "With his feathers fluffed up he can trap a layer of warmth between his feathers and his skin. That's why robins are such hardy little birds. He'll have no trouble keeping warm in all this snow."

She carefully reached into the box and lifted him out, holding his body gently but firmly between her fingers, so that his tiny legs stuck out through the gaps between her fingers.

"Goodbye, Lucky," said Evan.

"Goodbye," whispered Hannah. "Good luck."

For a moment, it seemed as if Lucky was looking directly at them, blinking his beady eyes.

Then Courtney opened her hand wide. Lucky stayed still, just for a second, as if he couldn't quite believe he was free. Then with a flutter of his wings he was off, soaring up and up, his breast a splash of colour lighting up the grey sky.

Evan and Hannah followed his flight for as long as they could, straining their eyes to follow him as he became a little speck that seemed to merge with the trees and the clouds. And then, the next moment, he was gone.

"He's free," said Evan, smiling.

8

"It's Christmas!" Evan shouted, leaping out of bed in excitement. And there, on the rug on the floor, was a lovely lumpy stocking, bursting with presents.

A moment later his door swung open and Poppy came in, dragging her stocking behind her in one hand and her bedraggled toy bunny in the other. "It's 'mistmas!" she declared.

Evan gave her a hug, feeling butterflies in his tummy as he thought about opening his stocking. "Let's go through to Mum and Dad," he said, "and open our stockings with them."

"Want open one now!" said Poppy determinedly.

"OK," said Evan. "Let's do one each, just us two together."

Poppy climbed up on to his bed, and Evan realized this was the first proper Christmas he'd shared with Poppy. Last year, she'd been too little to understand what was happening, but this year they felt like a team, sneakily opening a present before they went through to Mum and Dad.

Evan pulled out the top present of his stocking and ripped off the wrapping paper. "Awesome!" he said. "Look, it's a torch with loads of settings."

Then he burst out laughing. Poppy had opened a bottle of bubble bath and was clearly much more interested in her wrapping paper than the present.

"It's bubbles, Poppy," he said.

"Bubbles!" she repeated, her face lighting up.

"Right, come on, let's go and wake up Mum and Dad."

They crept down the corridor together, then leaped on to their parents' bed. "Wake up!" cried Evan. "It's Christmas!"

Dad groaned and looked over at the

clock. "It's six o'clock in the morning," he said. "Christmas doesn't start until seven."

"Nonsense," laughed Mum. "Come on, kids. Let's open those stockings."

Evan and Poppy spent the next half-hour unwrapping presents and laughing, as their parents put on silly Christmas hats and their mum put on cheesy Christmas songs.

"Can we open the presents under the tree now?" begged Evan.

"No!" laughed his mum. "We have to wait until Gran and Granddad are here. And you haven't even had breakfast yet."

"Hooray! 'Mistmas breakfast!" cried Poppy.

"I'm not sure that's an actual meal," Evan pointed out.

"Well," said his dad. "We can make it one. Who's for waffles and bananas with golden syrup?"

"Me!" Evan and Poppy cried.

"We need more Christmas songs, too," he said. "I'm not cooking without them."

As Dad toasted the waffles, Poppy and Evan brought down all their stocking presents to go through them again.

"This is my fav'rite," said Poppy, holding up a toy mouse.

"Which is yours, Evan?" asked Mum.

"I don't know," Evan replied. "Oh look – I missed one." There, at the bottom of his stocking, was something hard and square. He ripped off the wrapping paper. "That's brilliant!" he said, his eyes sparkling. It was a birdwatching book, with a picture of a robin on the front.

"This is great," said Evan, leafing through it.

"Just don't let Granddad see it," said Dad. "Or he'll be talking about birds all day! Now, at the table everyone. The waffles are ready!"

After breakfast, Evan and Poppy were sent outside into the garden to burn off some energy. Poppy took her toy mouse with her and began showing it round the garden, making little footprints with it in the snow. Normally, Evan realized, he'd be kicking a football around, seeing how much snow he could send up when the ball landed. But today he found himself standing by the hedge at the end of the garden, trying to stay as quiet and still as possible. Even in all the excitement of Christmas, he hadn't forgotten about the robin. He wondered how Lucky was doing, out there in all the snow. Perhaps it was a shock for him, after the comforts of the aviary. He wished he could see him, just one more time, to know how he was getting on. But although he spotted a blackbird and a pair of blue tits, there was no sign of the robin.

"Gran and Granddad are here," called his mum.

Evan ran in after Poppy and, with a

last glance over his shoulder, closed the back door behind him.

Gran and Granddad were already in the sitting room, admiring the tree. "It's even bigger than last year's," Gran pointed out. "And I love all the tinsel."

"That was Poppy," said Evan, giving them both a hug. "She just kept putting more and more on. None of us could stop her."

"It's pretty," Poppy insisted.

Everyone laughed. The tree did look as if it were drowning in tinsel.

"Now," said Granddad. "Who wants to open even more presents?"

"Me!" cried Poppy.

"Can we?" asked Evan, turning to Mum.

"Yes," laughed Mum. "I don't think we'll get any peace otherwise."

"I'll help hand them round," said Evan, crouching down by the tree. He picked out one for his mum and then passed another to his gran.

"Lovely manners," said Gran. "But you can open yours now, you know. We've got two for you this year. Here's the first one."

She handed him a big, squishy parcel. Evan knew *exactly* what it was. "Thanks, Gran!" he said, pulling out a big sloppy green jumper. "I wonder where you got this from?" he said, jokingly. Gran's knitting was legendary in their family. She was very rarely seen without her knitting needles.

"And here's your other one," Gran went on. "I have a feeling you're going to like it." She handed him a slim parcel, covered in holly leaf wrapping paper.

Evan felt really nervous before opening it. This was the parcel he'd been tentatively feeling ever since the presents had gone under the tree. He really hoped it was the computer game he'd asked for. . .

He pulled off a tiny scrap of paper and peeked inside. "Yes!" he cried, punching the air. "Thank you! Thank you so much." He gave Gran and Granddad a huge hug, grinning from ear to ear.

"Now, I think you've got a story to tell us," said Granddad. "We've been hearing all about a robin you rescued."

"It was amazing," said Evan. "We found Lucky, that's the robin, stuck in a glue trap on the last day of term, and then we called the RSPCA and they came to get him."

"And what happened after that?" asked Gran.

Evan smiled. He knew they'd heard the end of the story already. They were just letting him tell it.

"Then they let us go to the RSPCA centre and see our robin. And two days ago, they released him."

Out of the corner of his eye, Evan could see his mum smiling proudly at him.

"Oh, look," said Dad. "There's one more present for you under the tree."

"Really?" said Evan, as his dad passed it to him.

"I don't remember this one," he added, feeling its rough texture beneath the thin wrapping paper.

"Why don't you just open it and see what it is?" chuckled Granddad.

This time, Evan had no idea what it could be. And he still wasn't sure once he'd opened the present. . . It had a clear plastic dome on top, with a little dish underneath and a brass rod running through the middle. At the top was a little hook. "Oh!" he said suddenly, with a gasp of delight. "It's a bird feeder, isn't it?"

"It is," said Dad. "It's one specially

designed for robins. Apparently they have trouble landing on bird feeders, so they usually feed on the ground. But this one is easy for robins to feed from. And we've bought a bag of mealworms and waxworms, too, which they love, and some bird cakes, filled with seeds. Now your robin will be able to stop by for a snack whenever he likes."

"Wow! Thanks!" he said. "Now maybe I'll see Lucky again!"

9

"Can we fill the bird feeder now?" asked Evan.

"We'd better have lunch first," said Mum. "My turkey is just about perfect."

Evan thought lunch would last for ever – he couldn't wait to hang up his bird feeder. As soon as it was over, he asked again.

"Of course you can," said his dad. "The bird food is in the cupboard under the stairs. Actually on second thoughts," he added, getting up, "I'll help you open it. I know what you're like – you'll be so excited you'll rip it open, and then we'll have mealworms everywhere."

Dad opened up the packets and Evan shook out the waxworms and mealworms into the little dish at the bottom of the feeder. Then Evan pulled on his new woolly jumper from his gran and ran for the door.

"Where are you going?" asked Granddad.

"I want to hang it up now, in the garden," said Evan.

"Don't you want to play with your new computer game first?" asked Mum. "You've been so excited about it."

Evan looked at the computer game, still lying in the box, then back at the bird feeder in his hand. "No," he said. "I definitely want to do this first. Do you want to come too, Poppy?"

But Poppy was completely absorbed
by her new set of saucepans, making an
imaginary pie out of scraps of wrapping
paper.

"I'll come with you," said Granddad.
"Then we can work out the best place to
put it."

They stood in the snowy garden
and Evan felt a rush of excitement as
he thought about where to hang it. At
the back of his mind, he couldn't help

thinking that if he filled the bird feeder and always kept an eye on it, then maybe, just maybe, he'd catch another glimpse of the robin.

"How about from this tree?" Evan suggested. It was right next to the house, so he'd easily be able to spot any birds from the window.

"That's probably a bit too close to the window," said his granddad. "Sometimes birds get confused and fly straight at the windowpane, and we don't want that happening. How about that tree, over there?"

Granddad pointed to a tree at the other end of the garden. "It won't be too windy there as it's in a sheltered spot, and it's far from the windows, but you'll still be able to get a great view of any birds that come to visit." He nodded with satisfaction. "And," he went on, "even more importantly, the tree doesn't have any low branches, so you won't get any predators like cats pouncing on the birds."

"Perfect!" said Evan. "Shall we just hang it with the hook? It looks like it might fall off if there's too much wind. Shall I go and get something to hang it with?"

"You don't have to worry about that," said Granddad, chuckling.

They walked over to the tree and Evan smiled as Granddad pulled a penknife and a ball of twine out of his pocket.

"What else do you have in there?" Evan asked.

"Everything I might need," said Granddad, cutting the twine with the knife and beginning to hang up the bird feeder. "I've got a compass, a notebook, a pen and a big hankie."

He jiggled his hand in his pocket some more. "Oh, yes," he said, pulling out some pieces of wrapping paper. "And Poppy's 'Christmas Pie' that I pretended to eat."

"I wondered how you'd managed to finish your bowl from her!" laughed Evan. "Oh, wow!" he added, looking up again. "You've done it!"

"Yes," said Granddad. "With my best boy scout knot, too."

Evan gazed for a moment at the bird feeder swinging gently in the breeze, then looked around to see if there were any birds eyeing it up.

"I think we'd better go in now," said Granddad. "It's getting chilly out here, and no bird is going to come along while we're gawping at the bird feeder."

"Oh, please can we stay?" begged Evan. "Just a little while longer."

Granddad ruffled his hair. "You've got to learn patience if you're going to become a proper birdwatcher," he said. "Give the birds time to realize the feeder is here, and give them some space to use it. Then you'll be amazed by how many come to visit your garden."

"Do you really think so?" asked Evan.

"I do," said Granddad. "You'll have to take proper care of it though. That means cleaning your feeder once a week. And we'd better get a drinking station, too.

That'll need cleaning once a day. And you have to move them about a bit, to stop any diseases from spreading."

"I can do that," said Evan. "What birds have you got in your garden, Granddad?" he went on, as they came back inside.

"We've got all sorts at home," Granddad replied. "Blue tits, great tits, starlings. My favourite are the long-tailed tits, though. They look like little balls of fluff on a stick. And they've got lovely pink colouring on their tummies, too."

"I think my favourite is always going to be the robin," said Evan.

"I expect it will be," his granddad replied. "And it's not surprising after you helped rescue one."

They pushed open the back door and Evan took off his boots, being careful to shake off the snow outside. He could hear new voices in the sitting room and raced through to find Hannah and her mum and dad sitting down on the sofa.

"Merry Christmas!" said Evan.

"Merry Christmas!" cried Hannah, getting up. "Guess what I got?"

"Your paints?" asked Evan.

"Exactly," said Hannah. "Real watercolours. There are twenty of them, and I've even been given a couple of new brushes – tiny ones so I can do really delicate strokes."

"Have you done any pictures yet?" asked Evan.

"I have," said Hannah proudly. "And it's for you."

Evan took the piece of paper she held out to him. Then he opened it up and gasped. "That's amazing," he said.

The whole of his family gathered

round to look. "It really is good, Hannah," said Evan's mum. "You're very talented."

Evan smiled at her. "It's Lucky, isn't it?" he asked.

"Of course it is," said Hannah. "Look," she said, pointing to the robin's feet. "I've even done his tag, too."

Evan gazed at the picture for a moment without saying anything. It really did look just like their robin. She'd done his curious little black eyes perfectly, and the blue-grey feathers around his red breast. Hannah had painted him on the ground on the snow, with his head cocked to one side.

"How did you remember him so well?" asked Evan.

"I don't know," said Hannah. "I think it's just how my memory works. If I shut my eyes tightly and think about him really hard, I can just picture him."

"Well, now I'll be able to remember him, too," said Evan, "every time I look at this picture. Thanks, Hannah. It's a great present."

"What about you? Did you get the computer game you wanted?"

"Oh, I did," said Evan. "I'd forgotten about that."

"How could you have forgotten?"

"Because *after* the computer game, I was given a bird feeder, and Granddad helped me hang it outside. Come and see!" he said excitedly.

They rushed through to the kitchen,

Hannah following behind Evan. "You can see it from the window," said Evan. "There might even be some birds already."

They went over to the window together.

"Look!" cried Evan. There was a blur of brown wings and a little robin landed on the bird feeder. They were just in time to see its head bob down as it picked up a worm in its beak, then it was off again, disappearing over the garden hedge.

"It was a robin!" said Evan. "It was definitely a robin. I saw its red breast. Did you see it, too?"

Hannah nodded, her eyes shining. "I did," she said. "Do you think it was him? Do you think it was Lucky?"

Evan paused for a moment. "I'm going to think that it is," he decided. Then he remembered his granddad's saying. "Let's make a wish," he said.

They both squeezed their eyes tight shut and wished.

"What did you wish for?" said Hannah.

Evan just smiled at her. "I can't tell you or it won't come true," he said.

Just then, Mum called out, "Christmas cake time! And bring through some plates, please."

"Hurry!" added his gran. "We're all starving for cake!"

Hannah laughed. "Coming!" she called back, making her way through.

Evan couldn't resist one more look out of the window. There was nothing on the bird feeder now and the winter sky was already darkening. He thought of the robin, out there in the snowy dark, and he was glad it would have somewhere to go to find food. Then he thought of his wish again – that the little robin would visit him every day.

The Real-Life Rescue

Although the characters and animals in this story are fictional, their story is based on a real-life rescue in which a robin got stuck on a glue trap.

The bird was found in a London street by two twelve-year-old boys on their way back from school. The boys noticed that the little robin was struggling and called the RSPCA. They then waited with the bird until Inspector Natalie Bartle arrived and managed to prise him away from the sticky mat.

Inspector Bartle said: "This poor little robin was a pitiful sight when I first arrived – very distressed and sticky all over. Without the caring attitude and diligence of these two boys, who knows how much longer it would have suffered. It just shows how cruel these traps can be. They catch any animal which happens along, and this robin was very lucky to escape."

Despite the loss of tail feathers, the robin survived and was taken to a wildlife centre where it was later released back into the wild.

A robin in the snow

Facts About Robins

- Young robins have a brown rather than a red breast.

- Robins are "omnivores". They eat anything from fruit and seeds to spiders and mealworms.

- The female robin builds the nest — usually among bushes or in holes in walls — and lines it with roots, moss, feathers and hair.

- Some robins have been known to nest in unusual places, such as sheds or old teapots!

- In winter, the robin puffs up its feathers to insulate its body against the cold.

Take a sneak peek at
another exciting story based
on a real-life animal rescue!

"So what game are we going to get, then?" Dad asked as they drove down the country lane into town.

"It's called *Ice Storm*," Lewis grinned. "I've played it round at Maddy's house and it's brilliant. You have to collect all these stars that give you superpowers, and the baddies throw icicles to try and freeze you."

Dad sighed. "I don't know why you don't do something useful, like read a book."

Lewis rolled his eyes. Whenever Mum had to go away to a sales conference, or

to visit Granny and Pops back in Jamaica,
he and Dad were stuck with each other all
weekend long. He loved his dad, but
all he ever did was work, and he seemed
to think that's all Lewis should do, too!
Yesterday, before she'd left, Mum had
suggested that they go into town and get
the game that Lewis had wanted for ages.
But Dad was even ruining that.

Lewis put his feet up on the car
dashboard and glanced at his dad. Dad

was long and lanky, like him, but that was about the only way that they looked the same. Lewis was like Mum, with chocolate-brown skin, dark eyes and afro hair. He liked wearing jeans and trainers, but Dad always wore smart clothes, even at the weekend. Dad's skin was white and freckly, and he had brown hair. Behind his sunglasses, Lewis knew that Dad had light blue eyes that twinkled when he smiled, but that didn't happen very often.

Dad glanced over at him. "Feet!" he warned Lewis immediately. Lewis gave an exaggerated sigh and put them down.

At least they were going to see Granddad tomorrow. Granddad was Dad's dad, and he was really fun. He was always telling Lewis exciting stories about his time in the Navy, or playing with Alfie, his old greyhound dog. Granddad was as fun as Dad was serious.

Sometimes Granddad seems like the young one, and Dad the grumpy old man! Lewis thought, grinning to himself.

He wound down the window as they drove down the little windy country lane, covered with fields on both sides. The sun was shining brightly, and the air smelled like cut grass and holidays. School was just about to start again, but it didn't really feel like autumn yet. Lewis had had a brilliant summer. He and Mum had gone to stay in Cornwall with his best friend Maddy and her family – her mum and her big brother Stephen. They'd been fishing and crabbing, and eaten ice cream every day. Dad hadn't come because he hadn't been able to take any time off from work.

Lewis stared out of the window as

he remembered his holiday. But as he was thinking, a flash of black and white caught his eye. Something was lying at the side of the road. "Dad, stop!" he said, sitting up in his seat and straining to look out of the window.

"What?" Dad quickly pulled the car over to the side of the road. "Are you OK?"

"I saw an animal," Lewis said, unbuckling his seat belt. "It was on the road, it might be hurt."

"Lewis, we can't just stop—" Dad began to say, but Lewis was already getting out of the car.

Making sure there was nothing coming, he ran across the lane. At the end of a row of parked cars, there was a small animal, lying very still.

Please let it be OK, Lewis thought as he

crept towards it. *Was it a cat, or a dog?* It had a dark grey body, and a stubby grey tail. As Lewis stepped closer, it looked up, and Lewis gasped as he saw its face. It had black and white lines over a long snuffly nose. Its eyes were black and beady, and it had little black paws, with strong-looking claws.

"It's a badger!" Lewis called excitedly to Dad in the car. "I've never seen one in real life before."

"It's probably got fleas," Dad called

back. "Come on."

"We can't just leave." Lewis stepped closer. The badger was only small, and its beady, black eyes looked up at him fearfully. As Lewis got closer, it shuffled backwards towards the nearest car, dragging one of its back legs behind it.

"Look, Dad, it *is* hurt," Lewis said. "We have to help."

"OK," Dad sighed and Lewis heard him getting out of the car. But the sound of the car door shutting startled the young badger. Before Lewis could move, it disappeared right underneath a van that was parked nearby.

"Oh no!" Lewis gasped. "She's scared." He kneeled down and peered under the van. The badger peeped back at him. "Don't be afraid," Lewis said. "We want to help you."

"Lewis, we can't stay here all day, or

you'll never get your game," Dad said. "She'll come out when she's ready. She's a wild animal, not a pet. And you don't even know if she's a girl, anyway."

"She looks like a girl. And I don't care about the game!" Lewis insisted. "There must be *something* we can do. What about the rescue centre where Granddad got Alfie? They help animals, don't they?"

"The RSPCA?" Dad said. "Actually, that's not a bad idea. Hold on, I'll give them a ring."

Dad walked back to the car and Lewis sighed with relief. "It's going to be OK," he promised the badger. She just peered up at him and snuffled her nose again.

Lewis looked around for something he could give her. He spotted a clump of grass and went and collected a handful.

"Come on, Badger," Lewis said

soothingly as he kneeled down and held a long blade of grass under the van. The badger's snout wriggled as she sniffed at it, but she didn't come out. "Come and get the nice food," Lewis coaxed her.

But the badger just stared at him. Lewis studied her face. He couldn't believe he was so close to a wild animal. Her eyes were bright and intelligent, like she understood every word he said. She had a dark nose, with fine, white whiskers poking out from either side. Her stripes were perfectly straight, like they'd been painted on. She was beautiful!

"Badgers don't eat grass," Dad told him as he reappeared with his phone. "They eat worms and snails, things like that."

"Oh," said Lewis, coming out from under the van and scrambling to his feet. "What did the RSPCA say?"

Dad held out his phone and showed him the RSPCA's website on the screen. "I rang the emergency hotline and they said they'll send an officer out straight away. There's a rescue centre just outside town. I didn't even know it was there."

"I knew they'd help!" Lewis said happily. He sat down again and, to his surprise, Dad kneeled down next to him. They both peered under the van. The badger looked back, curiously.

"I think I'll call her Bramble," Lewis said.

"Bramble?" Dad looked surprised. "That's a nice name. What made you think of that?"

Lewis smiled. "Granddad said that now it's September, it's almost time to go blackberry picking again. Last year Archie got stuck in a bramble bush. It took ages to get him out!"

Dad laughed and shook his head. "That dog is a troublemaker!"

Lewis glanced under the van. The badger looked back, her snuffly snout poking out.

"It's OK, Bramble," Lewis told the frightened badger. "Help will be here soon."

Join the RSPCA!

You'll receive:

- **six issues of** *animal action* **magazine**
- **a brilliant welcome pack**
- **a FAB joining gift**
- **and a FREE gift with every issue.**

Go to: **www.rspca.org.uk/theclub**

Ask an adult to call:
0300 123 0346 and pay by debit/credit card.

ALL FOR £15!
(£22 OVERSEAS)